TIME FIX
and Other Tales of Terror

TIME FIX
and Other Tales of Terror
Don L. Wulffson

COBBLEHILL BOOKS
Dutton   New York

Library of Congress Cataloging-in-Publication Data
Wulffson, Don L.
Time fix and other tales of terror / Don L. Wulffson.
p.   cm.
Contents: By the book—The fortune-teller—Time fix—Crank call—Dream world —Captured on canvas—Class reunion—The hunted.
ISBN 0-525-65140-3
1. Horror tales, American.   2. Children's stories, American. [1. Horror stories.
2. Supernatural—Fiction.   3. Short stories.] I. Title.
PZ7.W96373Ti   1994   [Fic]—dc20   93-40184   CIP   AC

Published in the United States by Cobblehill Books,
an affiliate of Dutton Children's Books,
a division of Penguin Books USA Inc.,
375 Hudson Street, New York, New York 10014

Designed by Jean Krulis
Printed in the United States of America
First Edition   10   9   8   7   6   5   4   3   2   1

*Thanks to my editor for her help
in making this book possible*

Contents

1
By the Book

HENRY BLOUNT HAD always been an avid reader. Books had always held a certain magic for him. He could not have anticipated that that magic would, within a short time, change to horror—and prophesy his own death.

Perhaps if Henry had not gone to Jacoby's that lovely, crisp autumn morning, none of it would have happened. But that is a moot point, for there he was, bright and early, in old man Jacoby's Used & Rare Book Mart, browsing through musty works from days gone by. He flipped through the pages of a little-known collection of stories by Hawthorne. Lovingly, he examined an antiquated edition of the poetry of Emily Dickinson. He was tempted to buy it, but the price was high; too, he already had more than one collection of the poet's work at home.

Henry set the book aside, made his way to the back shelves of Jacoby's.

At first, nothing interested him. He knelt down. And there, on an almost floor-level shelf he saw it, touched it. Startled, disbelieving, he stared at the old leather-bound novel. He pulled it from the shelf, blew dust from the binding. The work was entitled *The Life and Death of Henry Blount—A Novel.* His hand trembling, he scanned a few pages. "What?" he blurted. "What!"

"Is something the matter, Henry?" called Sam Jacoby.

"This book!" exclaimed Henry.

Sam Jacoby wondered at his long-time customer. Henry was hurrying, and lurching a bit, as he made his way down the aisle toward the front of the shop. His face was in the book. His thick reading glasses were askew.

"What's wrong?" asked Sam.

"This book! That's what's wrong!" Henry said sharply. He slapped down the volume on the worn counter on which old Mr. Jacoby's wrinkled hands rested. "This novel. The title! Look at the title!" He turned the book, jabbed at the cover. "*The Life and Death of Henry Blount!* That's me, my name!"

"How strange," said Sam. "But certainly a coincidence." He fixed tired blue eyes on the book and opened to the inside cover. "Written by L. Calderhill. I'm not familiar with the author. Written in 1891. And it was—"

"Just ring it up!" Henry demanded, interrupting him.

He glanced at the price sticker, pushed a ten-dollar bill across the counter.

"Sure, Henry. Whatever you say."

Twenty minutes later, book in hand, Henry pushed through the front door of his house. He was hurrying into the study when he heard his wife's voice upstairs.

"Henry, that you?" called Sylvia from the bedroom. "Can you give me a hand, dear?"

Without answering, he made his way up the stairs and into the room. Clothes were neatly folded on the bed. Sylvia was on a stepladder in the closet, struggling with a suitcase. He vaguely remembered something about her going to San Francisco to visit her sister. But wasn't that next week?

She climbed down. "Can you help me with this, dear?"

Waving her aside, he pulled down the suitcase and set it on the bed. He wanted to tell her about the book. His mouth opened to speak.

"I think I should leave at about two," said Sylvia. "I want to beat the traffic. And I think I should have the tires checked before I leave, don't you? It's over a two-hundred-mile drive to San Francisco. And all those hills in that city! I should probably have the brakes checked, too. Think I should?"

"Yes," he mumbled.

"Angela called. Said they have an Autumn Arts Festival all week. That should be fun."

"I'm sure," said Henry. Sylvia was still prattling as he escaped, and hurried downstairs.

"Henry?" she called out from above, her voice muffled, indistinct.

"Got something to do," he said, and softly shut the study door.

All was quiet.

For a moment he felt guilty, and even a bit angry with himself. He had been rude to Sam, and now to Sylvia. All because of a silly book. He had gone off the deep end, gotten himself all upset. Over nothing.

Or was it nothing?

The old novel, its binding tattered and its pages yellowing, enticed him. It fascinated him, and troubled him to the core of his being.

He sat down, pushed his glasses higher on his nose. He opened the book and, with trepidation, began to read. Trepidation turned to fear. And with the turning of each page, his fear grew, changed to horror. The fictional character of the book was a boy who had grown up on a farm in Iowa (as Henry had!). The parents' names were Mildred and Zachary (his own parents' names!). At the age of eight, the boy had huddled with his parents in a storm cellar (just as he and his parents had) as a tornado had literally carried the house away from over their heads. Tough times had followed as the family struggled to rebuild the farm—and failed. And just like Henry and his parents, they had packed what they could and headed west, to California . . .

There was a gentle rapping at the door. Sylvia peeked in. "I'm off to the gas station and to do a few other errands," she said. Her brow furrowed as her eyes fixed on Henry. "Dear, your face is flushed. You look a bit ill. Are you okay?"

"I'm fine," mumbled Henry.

"You sure?"

"Yes," he said, forcing a smile.

"Be back in a while," said Sylvia.

Moments later, the car started up, backed out of the drive. Henry returned his attention to the book.

In California, the whole family had worked, doing whatever jobs they could—from factory work to picking fruit and vegetables. (How clearly Henry remembered those days!) Then they had opened a small store. Life was better. At the age of seventeen, the main character had tried to enlist in the army, but had been turned down (just as Henry had!). He had never thought of college, but at eighteen, off to college he had gone. And at the age of twenty-six he had become a professor of literature (Henry's vocation!). Down to the last detail, it—the book—was his biography. But how—how could a book written more than a hundred years before—tell the story of his life? How?

His finger marking his place, he closed the book. With

his shirtsleeve, he wiped sweat from his brow. He stared at the musty volume. For a moment he was tempted to turn to the final page—to find out how it all ended.

Tires crackled in the driveway. Henry parted a curtain; Sylvia had returned. Distressed, desperate to talk to her, he met her as she made her way through the back door into the kitchen.

"Henry, what in the world is wrong?" she asked, setting parcels on the kitchen table. "You look like you've seen a ghost. You . . ."

Pacing, agitated, he explained about the book. Again and again he rapped the cover with his knuckles for emphasis.

"Well, I admit it's very odd," she said, "and very interesting. But I think you're getting all upset for no reason. None at all."

He scowled.

"Now, really, Henry, be rational about this."

"But almost every detail is the same!"

"You say 'almost.' So there must be differences."

"Well, some," he admitted. "But—"

" 'But' nothing. There *are* differences, and this is certainly *not* your life story. It's a novel; it's fiction."

Henry was thumbing back through the book. "Listen to this," he said. He began to read: " 'His father was a man whose face was all wrinkles, a dirty crosshatch of hard furrows as unyielding as the rocky ground he plowed.'" He closed the book. "That describes my father's face to a T!"

Sylvia smiled. "And probably that of any Iowa farmer —at least in those times."

Henry said nothing. He thumbed back to an earlier page. "Well, how about this?" he exclaimed. "A tornado hit the farm when the kid was eight—which was how old I was, I think, when the tornado hit."

"You think?" she parroted.

"Well, I'm pretty sure that's how old I was."

Sylvia smiled. "Henry, dear, how many Midwestern farms have been hit by tornadoes in, say, the last century?"

He shrugged. "Well, hundreds, I guess."

"Exactly my point. A tornado wiping out a farm, in any story about the Midwest, is the kind of thing you'd *expect* to be part of the action. Do you see my point?"

"Yes, but—"

"No *buts* about it," she said, interrupting. "Now put that book out of your head. Forget about it."

He sighed.

Sylvia gently pried the book from his hands. "I agree this *is* quite intriguing," she said, "but I am *not* going off for almost a week, leaving you like this, working yourself into a tizzy over absolutely nothing."

He frowned, his eyes on the book.

"I'm going to put it aside—put it away—until I get back next week. And I want you to promise me you won't even so much as think about it until then." She smiled. "Promise?"

He nodded begrudgingly.

"Good!" she exclaimed. She gave him a peck on the cheek, then headed out of room with the book in hand.

Henry kept his promise until midmorning of the next day. He worked in the yard. He paid the bills. He tried to watch TV. His mind wandered. He was bored. Distracted. His mind was on one thing.

The book was easy enough to find. Sylvia had stashed it in a hall cabinet, under a stack of towels. Within minutes, Henry was on the phone to the New York publisher of the work. His voice quavering, he described the situation to a confused editor, insisted that she explain how and why his life had somehow been twisted into the pages of a novel. After putting Henry on hold for what seemed an eternity, the editor finally came back on the line. In checking the files, she told him, she had found that the author was deceased, the book was out of print, and the story had been written long before Henry had been born. Any similarity between the story and his own life was purely coincidental.

Flustered, suddenly angry, Henry hung up on the woman. He snatched up the book. He paced, wandered from room to room, then headed upstairs to the bedroom. He sat down heavily in an easy chair beside the bed. He began reading again, rapidly turning the pages.

Spellbound, he read for an hour, then two. And on into early evening. Soon all was black outside. A cold, gusting wind began to whine.

I don't want to read this, agonized Henry. But still he continued on. He had to finish the book. He had to find out how it ended.

He read on. He came to the last page. His eyes opening wide, magnified behind his thick glasses, he read: *From below came the sound of breaking glass, then of heavy, drumming footfalls slowly ascending the stairs. In horror, Blount put down the phone. Rising slowly, he searched futilely for something with which to defend himself. The door of the bedroom squawked open and a spectral figure stepped into the half-lit gloom. A pistol barked, shattering the silence. Henry Blount, a bullet in his heart, was dead before he hit the floor.*

Henry was gasping for breath as he read this. He shut the book. He tried to calm himself. *Not possible!* he muttered. He pushed the book aside. *Coincidence! What other explanation can there be?*

For a long while he sat, staring into space. He picked up the phone. He would call Sylvia. Or if not her, someone else. Talking to her—to anyone—about the book would help him, would help ease his terror.

The phone was in his hand as he suddenly went rigid with fear. From below came the sound of breaking glass, then of heavy, drumming footfalls slowly ascending the stairs . . .

2 The Fortune-teller

ALL AFTERNOON Helen had been knocking on doors until she was tired and discouraged. She had not expected to get rich selling magazines, but she did expect to sell more than two subscriptions in almost four hours of work. She wanted to cry.

By now her sales pitch had become automatic. "The Magazine Guild has a really wide selection of magazines," Helen was saying to the man at the door. "And they are offering these special low prices for only a short period of time. For example, the regular price for—"

"I have all the magazines I need," the man interrupted.

"But there's a 10 percent discount on the price of any magazine you're already getting," Helen added desperately.

"Not interested. Sorry," the man mumbled. His face disappeared behind the closing door.

"That's it! I quit!" Helen muttered. Tucking her order forms under her arm, she headed for the stairway, but then, with a heavy sigh, she stopped. There was one last apartment on the floor. This would be her final try, resolved Helen. She straightened up and pressed the doorbell.

She jumped back with a start. Almost before the bell rang, the door swung open and a tall, gray-haired woman appeared.

"Hello, my dear," said the woman. She smiled as if she knew Helen and had been expecting her.

For a moment Helen held her breath. The old woman looked harmless, but there was something odd about her.

"I'm . . . I'm selling magazines," Helen stammered, struggling to recall her sales pitch.

"How nice," answered the woman. "Won't you come in?"

"Come in?" asked Helen, surprised by the unexpected invitation.

"Of course, dear. Please come in."

Helen hesitated. Then, as if her legs were being controlled by someone else, she walked into the apartment. The woman closed the door softly and led Helen into a dimly lit room.

"I'm Madam Dolores. Please sit down." She gestured toward some high-backed chairs grouped around a heavy oval table. "Poor dear, you look tired. Can I get you a cold drink?"

"Oh, no. That's all right," said Helen, sitting nervously on the edge of a chair. "I . . . I don't want to put you to any trouble."

"No trouble at all," said the woman, smiling brightly. Her voice trailed off as she left the room.

Helen settled back in the chair and tried to relax. The room was dark and old-fashioned. She thought, *this is like an apartment from the last century.* The room had green velvet drapes, faded rugs, and funny little lamps. Helen noticed the tabletop, which was decorated with a diagram of the zodiac. *The old lady must be a fortune-teller or something*, she thought, running her fingers over the colorful, wheel-shaped design.

Curious now, Helen studied the room more closely. Against one wall stood a small, strangely tilted table, and on a large wooden chest next to her lay a deck of oversize cards. Gingerly, Helen picked up the cards and turned one over.

"Are you interested in tarot?" a soft voice asked. Startled, Helen turned to see the old woman placing a tray on the table.

"No. I mean, I don't know anything about it," Helen stammered.

"Really, it's just a game." The woman smiled and sat down beside Helen.

12

"Thank you for the snack," Helen said as she took a sip of ginger ale.

"Tarot cards, Ouija boards, crystal balls, all those things are just toys," continued the old lady. "Amusing to a true psychic, but nothing more."

"Are you a fortune-teller?" asked Helen.

The woman laughed oddly. "You might say that I used to be. I was known as Madam Dolores, and some people called me a fortune-teller, but those days are over now."

"How did you become a fortune-teller?" Helen asked, taking a small bite of cookie.

"Oh, you don't want to hear about that," said the old woman. "You came to sell magazines, not to listen to an old story."

"No, really, that's okay," said Helen, growing less nervous and more curious by the minute.

"Well, I'll tell you what," said the woman. "If you're kind enough to listen to my story, then I promise to buy some magazines."

"Okay," laughed Helen. "It's a deal."

"I wasn't much older than you are now," said the woman. "My sister, Victoria, and I were spending the summer in New Orleans with our grandfather. A few days before we were to go home, we went into the city. On Bourbon Street we passed a strange little shop. It was a tiny place. I can see it to this day. Red letters in the window said PALMS READ AND FORTUNES TOLD. Victoria dared me to go in. I wasn't really afraid, but I felt silly. I'd never been in a place like that before. But Vicky—Victoria—kept teasing me, so finally I knocked.

"An old woman opened the door and told me to come in. We sat down at a table, and she began to lay out the tarot cards. As she worked, she became more and more excited. Her eyes were like two green flames. She said that I would acquire great wisdom and true knowledge of the occult. Of course, I didn't know what to say to such a thing. I was just a young, foolish girl.

"The woman filled a cup with tea and asked me to drink it. When I finished, she told me to look at the pattern left by the leaves. To this day I've never forgotten what I saw. Inside the cup was a perfectly shaped question mark. When I asked her what it meant, she smiled strangely and said I would have to return the next day to find out."

"Did you go back?" Helen asked softly.

The woman nodded. "Yes, I went back. I went alone. I didn't want Victoria or anyone else with me. But the shop was closed. I knocked and knocked, but no one answered. I didn't know what to do, so finally I went into the shop next door. I asked the owner if he knew when the old woman would return. His reply was the answer to all my questions and the beginning of my new life."

"What did he say?" asked Helen breathlessly.

"The man laughed at me. 'When will she return?' he asked, as if I were crazy. 'That old woman's never coming back. She's dead! She died three or four weeks ago.' "

Helen gasped. "I don't understand. You mean—?"

"Yes," interrupted the old woman. "My fortune had been told by a dead woman. I had already gained true knowledge of the occult. My fortune had come true."

"And that's why you became a fortune-teller yourself?" asked Helen.

The woman nodded.

"That's the weirdest story I've ever heard," Helen whispered. "But it must have been some kind of a trick. The shopkeeper and the old woman were probably in on it together."

For a moment the woman looked at Helen, her face expressionless. Then her mouth broadened into a warm, soft smile.

"Yes, I'm sure you're right. It must have been some kind of trick," she said. Suddenly her smile turned to easy laughter.

"Dear me," said the woman, putting her hands together. "I've kept you listening to this old story all this time, but you came to sell magazines. A bargain is a bargain. I promised to buy some."

"Here's the list of magazines and prices," said Helen. She handed the woman an order form and a pen. "Just check the magazine you'd like to subscribe to."

The woman scanned the form briefly. Then she filled it out and checked several boxes. "I'll take those three," she said, handing the paper and pen back to Helen.

"Oh, thank you," said Helen. She glanced quickly at the check marks on the form and rose with a smile.

"It was my pleasure, dear," said the woman. "Here, let me show you out."

"You don't have to pay until your first magazines arrive," said Helen on the way to the door.

"That will be just fine, dear." Madam Dolores opened the door. "Just fine."

"And thank you again for the ginger ale and cookies . . . and the story."

"Oh, you're quite welcome. Good-bye," said the fortune-teller as she softly closed the door.

Helen bounded down the stairway. *Well, at least I made one good sale today,* she told herself. *Everybody says no to me all day, and then I sell three in one place.*

"Oh, darn it," Helen said to herself. She had stopped at the bottom of the stairs and was studying the order form. "She forgot to sign the order."

Helen turned and ran back up the stairs. She knocked on the woman's door, but there was no answer. She waited, then rang the bell. Still nothing. She knocked again.

"There's no one there," said a man passing down the hall.

"What do you mean?" asked Helen as a sudden feeling of uneasiness came over her.

"I mean there's nobody there."

"But the old lady . . . ?" Helen's voice trailed off. "What about the old lady?"

"Sorry. Guess you didn't know. The old gal passed away three or four weeks ago."

"That's impossible!" shouted Helen.

"Sorry to have to be the one to tell you," said the man kindly. "Guess you knew her, huh?"

Helen stared in horror at the man. Her mind was spinning.

"Did you know her?" asked the man.

But Helen couldn't answer. She felt the hairs rise on the back of her neck. Slowly she turned back to the door. *It's not possible*, she told herself. *It's not.* She listened numbly to the strangely distant sound of her own fist pounding on the fortune-teller's door.

3
Time Fix

ELLIOT FELLER LEANED back in his chair and smiled to himself. He felt good. He felt cocky. And most of all, he felt like laughing—laughing at all those who had laughed at him for so long.

For eleven years he had been teaching at Benton University. For eleven years he had taught students who could not appreciate his genius. For eleven years he had experimented, working endless hours, giving every bit of energy and thought to his project. And the others had just laughed and sneered at his work. But now it was his turn to laugh, his turn to sneer.

There was a timid knock at his office door.

"Come in," Feller said, swiveling around in his chair.

Andy Maldonado, his lab assistant, looked in nervously.

"It's almost 2:30," said Maldonado, "and they're all waiting for you. The reporters, the other professors, everybody has been waiting for almost half an hour, and they're getting angry, sir."

"Let them," sneered Feller. "Let them be angry. Let them wait!"

"But Dr. Feller, they . . ."

"Tell them I'm busy, but I'll be there as soon as I can."

"Okay, Doctor," mumbled Maldonado, closing the door softly.

Idly, Feller began sorting out papers and tossing them into his briefcase. He paid them scant attention. His mind was elsewhere, on the past, on all that had happened, on all he had endured.

When he had first come to the university, the other scientists had been excited about his theory. He had theorized that it was well within the realm of possibility to design a television that could pick up broadcasts from other time periods. Because time is nonlinear, it was possible, he had explained, to intercept television signal waves coming from both the past and the future. Using high-frequency time fixes, people would be able to see shows broadcast before they were born or long after they were dead and gone.

Theories are one thing. Proof—the kind of proof that

people can see with their own eyes—is something else. And soon, because Feller had no such proof, people had begun to lose interest in his work. Then, as the years passed, they had begun to laugh at him. He was a crackpot—a mad scientist wasting his life away down in his laboratory, a frustrated man trying to invent the impossible.

At times, Feller himself had begun to doubt that he would ever succeed. But he had never given up. He had worked on and on.

And then it happened. Two weeks ago the cross lines on the screen had formed a picture. The hair had stood up on the back of Feller's neck. His breath had come in shallow gasps. The world he saw on the screen was something neither he nor anyone else had ever seen before. Ecstatic, Feller realized that the images that flickered before him were coming from the future.

He was soon fast at work setting the time lock on different frequencies, flipping the image on the screen from the past to the future. One moment he was looking at a show broadcast in 1950, then a minute later he was watching the evening news in the year 2000.

Seeing broadcasts from the past was interesting, but it was seeing the future that electrified his imagination. Mostly, he tuned in the news. He was astounded by some events, such as Canada and the United States becoming one country in the year 1999. Two years later, Africa was ripped apart in a terrible war. By 2142 freight buses were traveling to and from Europe *under* the Atlantic Ocean, by tunnel!

An interesting problem was the fact that the language changed over the years. As he tuned in further and further into the future, Feller found it harder to understand the news because new words and accents were turning English into a foreign language.

The language wasn't the only thing that changed. Television, itself, was very different. Commercials were gone, and hundreds of channels were in use. And, most amazing, viewers could take part in TV programs. Their own sets had special remote control equipment that let them participate directly in quiz shows or electronically project their images into movies to become one of the characters.

Feller dragged his thoughts back to the present and looked at his watch. It was a quarter to three. A faint smile passed across his face. *I guess I've kept them waiting long enough*, he told himself.

Feller rose. He pulled on his suit jacket and snatched up his briefcase. Then, with a sudden feeling of excitement, he headed out of his office and down the three flights of stairs to his laboratory.

As he had expected, an angry and restless group greeted him as he pushed through the doors into the lab. But if the reporters and professors had expected an apology for keeping them waiting, they were dead wrong. A twisted smile on his face, Feller ambled slowly to the center of the room and raised his hand. The droning hum of angry voices was quickly replaced by silence.

Feller's opening remarks were brief and formal and coldly arrogant. He quickly outlined the theory behind his project, his many years of experimentation and testing, and the many hardships he had suffered at the hands of those who doubted and downgraded his work. He then described his recent breakthrough and some of the incredible things he had viewed on the miniature screen.

Feller paused. He raised his head, seeming to look down on the faces that surrounded him. "I am sure, ladies and gentlemen," he said, "that you are much more interested in what I have to show you than in what I have to say."

With a wag of his finger, he gestured for Maldonado to activate the machine. When a picture began to materialize, Feller took up the controls and motioned the reporters and professors forward.

"Ladies and gentlemen," he grinned, "it's Tuesday, November 3, 2065. Time for the six o'clock news."

Silently, the group pressed forward and with great excitement strained to see and hear the broadcast. The newscaster was discussing the upcoming marriage of Barbara Hansen, President of the United States. President Hansen was engaged to Barry LeBlanc, a prominent lawyer, and her wedding was expected to be the most important social event of the year.

The program continued with the weather report, and Feller turned down the volume. "Well, ladies and gentlemen, what'll it be? I can show you a movie from the year 2431. Or maybe you'd like a broadcast from Mars in 4211? You name it."

Setting and resetting the time-fix dial, Feller flashed an assortment of programs before his astonished audience. Comedy, news, concerts, plays, and children's programs were sampled. He smiled coldly as he watched the group's reaction. They were stunned. Suddenly, a voice cut the silence.

"Oh, how horrible!" A reporter was pointing open-mouthed at the set. Feller turned to the screen. A newscaster's throaty voice droned on about a disastrous war in Turkey while the camera scanned the shattered remains of a city after a nuclear attack.

A tall men with red hair spoke up, a troubled expression on his face. "Dr. Feller, if it is possible for us to see into the future, is it also possible for us to change it?" asked the man. "I mean, we have just seen a nuclear war in Turkey. Could we, knowing about it in advance, have prevented it?"

Feller studied the man. "I wouldn't know, Dr. Hart. I guess that's just something we'll have to find out."

"Dr. Feller," interrupted a woman who had been scribbling in a notebook. "You've shown us the distant future. But how about the *near* future. May we also have a look at that?"

"Of course," smiled Dr. Feller. "Let's have tomorrow's news."

Maldonado turned up the volume.

The broadcast was not a very dramatic one. The newscaster rambled on and on about the events of the day, the bits and pieces of stories weaving into a familiar pattern. In twenty-four hours, nothing had really changed. Tomorrow's news seemed much like today's.

Suddenly, there was a gasp, and a hush fell over the audience. Every eye was glued to the set.

". . . a great loss to the world of science," the newscaster was saying. "Only yesterday Dr. Feller had unveiled his time-fix television, our feature story on the eleven o'clock news last night. The car, according to reports, turned over after striking another vehicle at approximately 5:30 P.M. Dr. Feller was pronounced dead last night on arrival at the hospital. The second occupant of the vehicle has not been identified, pending notification of next of kin. The driver of the otherwise empty bus suffered only minor injuries."

Almost without pause, the announcer moved on to the next news item, leaving a breathless group staring at Feller.

Numb with fear, Feller stumbled to a chair and sat down. Maldonado nervously turned off the set, and the room filled with a heavy silence. Finally, Feller gazed up at the others.

"I was to have been on the road at 5:30," he said, his

voice a bottled-up whisper. "Maldonado was going to drive me to the airport. I was going to leave here right after this meeting to fly to Evansville to give a lecture. I was . . ."

Feller's voice trailed off. He scratched his head, lost in thought. Slowly, a smile spread across his face.

"I'm not moving from this chair," he announced. "Not until after five-thirty. I have no intention of dying. What I intend to do is to change one small piece of the future—my future."

His eyes gleamed wildly as his mind raced from thought to thought. "I'll take a later flight." He motioned to Maldonado. "Make the travel arrangements. And call Evansville. Do whatever needs to be done. But at five-thirty I'll be rooted to this chair!"

Feller glanced at his watch. Automatically, everyone in the room did the same. It was 4:42. A little less than an hour to go.

The minutes dragged on. No one moved. A reporter began scribbling some notes on a pad, then stopped as every eye turned toward the sound of his scratchings.

"Don't be nervous, ladies and gentlemen," Feller suddenly said. "I assure you I'll be alive and well at five-thirty."

Time moved slowly forward. 5:00 . . . 5:10 . . . 5:20 . . . 5:25 . . . 5:26 . . . 5:27 . . . 5:28 . . . 5:29 . . . . . . 5:30 . . . 5:31 . . .

Someone giggled. The room broke into tense, excited

chatter. Feller rose from his seat, looking triumphantly at his watch.

The room became quiet again. Every head turned toward Feller.

"Not only have you seen the future, ladies and gentlemen. You have seen it changed!" Feller announced, his face a mixture of relief, joy, and arrogance.

Though the short, twenty-minute flight to Evansville was a smooth and uneventful one, Feller felt unusually tired and shaky as he disembarked from the plane. As he entered the lobby of the small air terminal, he tensely scanned the crowd for a familiar face. *Where's Dr. Ling?* he asked himself, wondering if the man had forgotten to meet him.

Then he noticed a young woman a few feet away who seemed to be staring at him. Smiling, the young woman approached.

"Excuse me. Are you Dr. Feller?" she asked.

Feller nodded.

"I'm Diane Hinden, Professor Ling's assistant. After you missed your earlier flight, Dr. Ling wasn't able to come himself."

"Well, I had good reasons for taking a later flight," Feller snapped. Then, seeing her surprised look, he added in a more pleasant tone, "It's been quite an afternoon."

"Do you have any other luggage?" she asked.

"No, just these," said Feller, picking up his briefcase and overnight bag.

"Well, right this way, then," the woman said. "My car's parked right out in the lot."

"How was your flight?" she inquired as she started the car and backed out of the parking slot.

"Fine. Fine," replied Feller. He felt tired and uncomfortable. Though the terror he had felt only a short time earlier had passed, a dull feeling of uneasiness still tugged at his insides. He tried to relax, settling back in the seat as the car picked up speed and entered the flow of traffic on the highway.

Feller glanced at his watch. Almost 6:30. *It's all over now*, he told himself. *There is nothing to be afraid of.*

The young woman was talking again. "Your flight made good time," she said. "We'll be at Dr. Ling's in time for dinner. He's a real stickler about time. Dinner at six, no matter what."

"What are you talking about?" Feller felt a tug of panic. "It's way past six. It's almost six-thirty!"

Hinden laughed. "You forgot to set your watch back."

"My watch back?" Feller asked numbly, almost gagging with fear.

"Sure, when you crossed the state line, the time zone changed. It's an hour earlier here. Hey! Are you all right?"

She took her eyes from the road and stared at Feller. He had gone white with terror.

Feller screamed, but he never felt the impact of the oncoming car that sent them hurtling upside down into the path of a skidding bus.

4
Crank Call

THOUGH OLD-FASHIONED in his ways and often a bit absentminded, Fred Ross had been a pillar of society in the little town of Franklin Heights. He had served as the head librarian for thirty-nine years, since the day the Franklin Library had opened. In his younger days, he had been a volunteer fireman and, at the age of seventy-four, was in his third term on the town council.

It was during a council meeting that Fred Ross had died. Shortly after the meeting began, he had suddenly started gasping for breath. Clutching his chest, he had collapsed and before paramedics arrived, he was dead of a heart attack.

The funeral was held three days later, on a wet, slate-gray morning. A great many people in Franklin Heights attended. Fifteen-year-old Mark Thompson was there. His mother made him go, and he had talked some of his friends into going too, though none of them had really known Mr. Ross that well.

That evening, Mark invited them over. They gathered in the basement, which was one of their favorite hangouts. The basement had been made over into a game room—complete with TV, video games, a stereo, pool table, and old but comfortable furniture. Usually the place was alive with activity. Instead, the teenagers just sat about glumly. It was as though the funeral had brought the whole day to a dreary standstill. The funeral, and the death of Mr. Ross, seemed to be the only thing the kids could talk about.

"Wasn't it all kind of gross?" said Cheryl Hayes, slumped in a beanbag chair. "I mean, wasn't it awful seeing Mr. Ross lying there so waxy-looking in that coffin?"

Leticia Ramos glanced down at her arms. "Yeah," she said, "I still get goose bumps. Boy, he looked scary!"

Mark was listlessly tossing darts at the dart board. "I still can't believe it," he said. "It's hard to believe he's actually dead. I saw him down at the drugstore just last weekend, and he looked healthy enough. For an old person, I mean."

"Well," said Leticia, "I guess heart attacks can happen real suddenly when you're old."

"They don't only happen to old people," said Cheryl.

"My mom once knew a lady whose son had a heart attack when he was only fourteen."

"Fourteen!" exclaimed Paul Desmond, a worried expression coming over his face. "Wow! I'm gonna really start taking care of my health. Jogging in the morning, push-ups at night . . ."

"You're so self-centered," said Leticia, interrupting him. "How can you even think of yourself at a time like this? A man has died. He was buried today." Tears welled up in her eyes. "Doesn't that mean anything to you? Anything at all?" She sniffed, brushed a tear from her cheek.

Paul sneered. "I can't believe it. The human faucet is dripping again for the one millionth time. Turn it off, willya, Leticia?"

"Oh, just leave her alone, Paul," said Cheryl. "At least Letty cares about people. That's a lot more than you can say."

Paul frowned. "I *do* care about people. But I'm not going to start blubbering 'cause old man Ross is dead. And to tell you the truth, I'm getting sick of talking about the funeral. Going on and on about Mr. Ross and about him being dead and stuff is getting on my nerves."

"I agree," said Cheryl. "Let's think about more positive things. Let's talk about Mr. Ross when he was alive."

"No!" exclaimed Leticia. "Let's not talk about him at all, alive or dead."

"Why not?" said Mark. He tossed a last dart at the

board. "That's exactly what you should talk about, about the person when he was alive. It's better that way. We're supposed to remember people as they were when they were alive and well. Otherwise, all we'd think of would be their waxy, wrinkled, ugly old bodies lying in those coffins."

Leticia slapped a hand against her knee. "Cut it out, Mark! Stop talking like that!"

Mark grimaced. A silence settled over the room.

Paul shrugged. "Well, let's do *something*, you guys."

Cheryl began leafing through a TV magazine. "Anything good on the tube?" asked Mark. Cheryl shook her head. "Nothing worth watching."

"Let's go out, then, and hang out somewhere," said Mark.

Leticia turned her head toward the basement's one window. "Too dark and cold, and it's starting to drizzle again. But how about playing some video games?"

"Nah," said Mark, bored. "We've played those stupid things at least a million times. Besides—" He stopped himself at the sound of footsteps coming down the stairs. His mother snapped her handbag shut as she entered the room.

"Listen, Mark," said his mother. "I'm leaving with your father now to visit Aunt Elaine. You kids can all stay here, but I want you to keep out of trouble. All right?"

"Sure, Mom."

"We'll be home at about midnight."

"See ya," said Mark as his mother headed back upstairs. He settled down in a well-worn easy chair. His eyes came to rest on the basement extension phone beside him on a table. "Hey, I've got an idea," he said suddenly. "Let's make some crazy phone calls!"

"I don't know," said Leticia. "I'm really not in the mood."

"It's better than just sitting around all bored and depressed," said Cheryl.

"That's for sure!" exclaimed Paul. "I think it's a great idea!" He turned toward Cheryl. "Remember that time you did the crank call in your English accent?"

"Yeah, that was a scream."

"Up to trying it again?"

"Sure." She laughed. "Now'd be a bloody good time to try it, eh, blokes?" she said in an English accent.

Chuckling, Mark began flipping through a phone book. He stopped on a page at random, then let a finger travel down the listings of names and numbers. His finger stopped. "Ferrin!" he announced. "It's Greg Ferrin. His mother's a real grouch."

"Sure is," said Leticia. "Last year she called up my mom and yelled at her because we were playing music too loud at my brother's birthday party."

"Well, then it's time to give *her* a call!" laughed Mark, handing the receiver to Cheryl, then punching in the numbers.

Cheryl paced back and forth, anxiously waiting for someone to answer.

"Hello?" said a harsh female voice.

Cheryl grinned. "Ah, yes," she said, using her English accent. "Have I reached the Ferrin residence?"

"Yes."

"Am I speaking to Mrs. Ferrin?"

"Who is this? Who's calling?"

" 'Tis Penelope."

"What? Who?"

"Penelope Smithers, your English cousin, calling from jolly old England."

"I don't have any cousins in England," said the woman sharply.

"Are you sure?"

"Yes, and I'm quite sure you're just some stupid teenager harassing me. You ever do this again, and I'll call the police." Cheryl jumped as Mrs. Ferrin hung up with a bang.

Paul laughed. "Well, from what I could hear, you sure blew it, Cheryl. She knew almost from the start you were a fake."

Cheryl made a face. "Well, I thought I was pretty good."

"She sounded great," said Leticia, coming to her friend's defense. "She sounded real English to me."

"Let's see how good *you* are, Mr. Hotshot," Cheryl said

to Paul, handing him the phone receiver. "You try one."

"Okay, how about my Martian routine?"

"You've got to be kidding," scoffed Cheryl. "Everyone in Franklin Heights has gotten that one from us by now."

"The funniest time we did it was to Mr. Ross," said Paul. "He actually fell for it. That's one of the things I'm gonna miss most about him. No one was more fun in a crank call."

"Well," said Mark, "we still have Mrs. Ross. And she's even easier to fool than he was. In fact, I think maybe she's even daffier than he was."

"Oh, stop making fun of her," said Leticia. "She acts the way she does because she's old. I feel sorry for her, especially now that her husband is gone and she's all alone. She doesn't have any children. Who's she going to talk to now?"

Mark grinned. "How about . . . us?"

"Yeah. Yeah!" exclaimed Paul. "I have a fantastic idea. Why don't I call her up now and say I'm her dead husband talking to her from beyond the grave? I bet she'll believe it."

Leticia stared at him in disgust. "That's a terrible, cruel idea! You'll scare her to death."

"How could you even think of such a thing?" asked Cheryl.

"What's the big deal?" laughed Paul. "We may get her going for a minute. But she's so out of it she'll probably forget about it the second after she hangs up."

Mark pushed up from the chair and put his arm

around Cheryl. "Come on, Cheryl, be a sport. It'll be a lot of fun."

Cheryl pushed his arm away. "You have a pretty weird idea of fun."

"Yeah, that's true," he said. He turned to Paul. "You game, man?"

"Sure am."

"But I'll be the one to talk, not you."

"Why not me?"

" 'Cause," said Mark, "I'm good at making my voice sound scary. And I won't laugh in the middle like you did last Halloween when we did our space invaders routine to Mrs. Jenkins."

"Hey, calling Mrs. Ross was *my* idea, remember?"

"Yeah, but I'll do it *right*."

"You guys are both sick," said Cheryl.

Mark chuckled as he opened the phone book. "Here it is," he said. "Fred and Jessica Ross."

"You're not really going to do it?" exclaimed Leticia.

"Watch me," said Mark, picking up the phone. He turned to Paul. "Or maybe you're right, Paul. You thought of it, so you can do it, if you want."

"Nah, doesn't matter. You go on ahead."

Leticia turned to Cheryl. 'They're really going to do it!" she cried. She backed away. "You're both awful!"

Mark was already punching in the numbers.

Cheryl stared at him, openmouthed. "Don't!" she demanded.

"Quiet!" said Mark, holding up a hand for silence, his ear pressed to the receiver, listening as the phone rang. Paul edged closer, trying to listen. On the fifth ring, Mark was about to hang up. Then the sound of a phone being picked up sounded over the line.

"Hello?" said Mrs. Ross, her voice feeble and weary.

"Jes-si-ca?" said Mark in a deep voice, covering the mouthpiece with his shirt collar.

"Who is this?"

"Jessica, is that you?" said Mark, lowering his voice even more. "My dearest Jessica."

Mrs. Ross's voice was suddenly filled with alarm. "Who is this?" she said.

"Jessica, I've missed you so much. I've been so lonely these past three days. It's so cold down here . . ."

"Fred!" cried Mrs. Ross, her voice tremulous. "Fred? Fred! Fred, could it be you?"

"Jessica, I miss you."

Cheryl advanced on Mark, glowering. "Stop it, Mark!" she whispered angrily in his ear. "Hang up!"

"Leave him alone, Cheryl," said Paul.

Mark turned away from Cheryl, ignoring her. "Yes," he said into the mouthpiece. "Yes, it's Fred. I'm speaking to you from my new world."

Mrs. Ross's voice came through the receiver in a wailing shriek. "Fred, oh Fred! Come back to me! Please! I'm so lonely." Suddenly she began to sob.

"She believes it!" exclaimed Mark, covering the mouthpiece with his hand. "She actually thinks it's her husband from the grave!"

"Man," said Paul, "she will fall for anything!"

"That's enough!" cried Leticia, coming to stand beside Cheryl. "Hang up or I'll do it for you!"

Mark scowled. "Okay, I'll tell her I'm hanging up." He removed his hand from the mouthpiece and again spoke into the phone, switching to a deep voice. "Jessica, I must leave you now. Please take care of yourself. I love you and—"

"No!" screamed Mrs. Ross. "Fred, don't leave! Wait!"

Looking confused and a bit shaken, Mark slowly hung up the phone. He sat down heavily. All was quiet for a moment. He looked from Paul to Leticia to Cheryl.

"You're a monster, Mark Thompson," Cheryl blurted. "How could you be so mean?" She turned to Leticia. "Come on, Letty. Let's get out of here. There's no way I'm hanging around here with this creep."

"Calm down, willya?" said Paul. "Why be so upset? Anyone dumb enough to fall for a crazy call like that deserves whatever she gets."

"You're even worse than he is!" said Cheryl, eyes blazing.

"They're both total jerks," Leticia said. She turned and stalked up the stairs and out of the house, with Cheryl following.

For a long while the two were silent as they walked toward home. The streets were dark and empty, everything wet and glistening from the recent rain.

"I never thought they'd actually go through with it," said Leticia, breaking the silence.

"Well, they *did*," said Cheryl. "It was really cruel and stupid, but it's over and done with now, and I'm sure Mrs. Ross, after a while, will realize it was just a prank."

"What if she doesn't?"

"She will," said Cheryl.

"Mark can be such an idiot."

"I agree. Still, maybe we're being too hard on him. I doubt he would have done it if he had known she'd take him seriously."

"Well, he should have expected she'd react that way. On the day of her husband's funeral, especially." Leticia stopped, put her hand on her friend's arm. "Cheryl, there's only one way we—and Mrs. Ross—are going to feel better about all this."

"What?"

"Let's go over to Mrs. Ross's and tell her it was just a terrible joke."

"No! We can't do that. We'll all get into really bad trouble."

"We've got to. Mrs. Ross probably won't be able to sleep a wink all night if we don't."

Cheryl looked away for a moment, hugged herself against the cold of the night. She shrugged, then smiled at Leticia. "I guess you're right. I don't like it, but I guess it's really the only decent thing to do."

Feeling nervous, the girls headed off in the direction of Mrs. Ross's street. Twenty minutes later, they were standing in front of her house. Their nervousness mounted as they walked up to the front door and knocked softly, bathed in the frosty glow of a porch light. It seemed to be the only light that was on. They knocked again. There was no answer.

Cheryl let out a sigh of relief. "She's probably sleeping or gone off to visit friends. Probably hardly gave that stupid call a second thought." She smiled. "See! I told you there wouldn't be any problem."

"Well, just to make sure, let's come back tomorrow morning. Okay?"

"Sure. Why don't I meet you here at about ten o'clock?"

"Better yet," said Leticia, "why don't you sleep over tonight, and we can come back together."

"Great!" said Cheryl. "And maybe we can bake cookies."

"And rent a movie and eat the whole batch while we watch it!"

In a good mood, the girls set off for Leticia's house.

The next morning at the Ramos home, Leticia and Cheryl woke up to find Mrs. Ramos in the kitchen, drinking coffee and looking upset.

"What's the matter, Mom?" asked Leticia.

"I just got some bad news, Letty."

"What?"

"Poor Mrs. Ross passed away last night."

Leticia stared at her mother in disbelief. "Oh, no! Oh, Mom, you're kidding!"

"I'm sorry, dear. I can't believe it's true myself. It's like a nightmare—on the same day as her husband's funeral."

"But how did she die?" asked Cheryl. "What from?"

"The same thing that caused poor Fred's death—a heart attack. I guess she couldn't accept the fact that her husband was really gone. When it finally hit her that he was dead, the shock killed her." The woman glanced at her wristwatch. She rose from the chair and sighed. "Well, I've got to get your sleepyhead brother up. He's got a Little League game in thirty-five minutes. He's going to sleep right through it!"

Leticia and Cheryl stared at each other in shock as Mrs. Ramos headed up the stairs calling her son's name.

"It was the phone call that killed her," cried Leticia softly.

"I know," said Cheryl.

"They killed her!" said Leticia. "That horrible phone call of theirs!" Angrily, she pulled a windbreaker from a closet, then headed for the back door.

"Where are you going?"

"Mark Thompson's! Want to come?"

"I'll get my coat."

———

At the Thompsons' house, they found Mark and Paul sitting down in the basement game room. A single lamp cast an eerie, yellow glow. The boys looked up nervously at the approach of the two girls.

"You . . . !" exclaimed Leticia angrily, tearfully, struggling to find the right words.

"We've all heard the news, Letty," said Paul gloomily. "Don't start in on us, okay?"

Mark ran his hand through his hair. "Honest, we feel bad enough already." He grimaced, hung his head. "I feel sick about it. It's all my fault."

"No, it isn't," said Paul. "I was the jerk who thought of it."

"Yeah, but *I* was the one who *called* her." He gazed off into space. "Me! I *killed* her!"

"But you didn't mean to," said Paul. "You didn't mean any harm."

Cheryl sat down, wiped a tear from her cheek. "Unfortunately, that doesn't really change anything. She's dead, and there's nothing we can do to bring her back, to change what's happened. It's over."

"Why?" said Mark plaintively. "Why did I do it?"

No one answered. The four sat in silence, each privately brooding over the dark, disturbing chain of events.

The phone rang, shattering the silence.

Mark picked up the receiver. "Hello," he said softly.

There was a static-laced crackle over the line. And then

a ghastly, distant-sounding, unearthly voice: "Thank you. I appreciate what you have done. If it hadn't been for you, I would not be with my loving husband."

"No!" screamed Mark.

The voice continued: "I will be calling you again . . . and again . . . and again. To thank you." Suddenly the phone went dead, then a dial tone returned.

"Hello?" yelled Mark frantically into the phone. "Hello?" Staring at the others, he slowly hung up the phone.

"What's wrong?" asked Cheryl anxiously.

"Who was it?" asked Paul.

Mark's eyes were glazed with horror. "It was . . ." he said hoarsely, ". . . it must have been . . . a crank call. Must have been."

5
Dream World

DR. RICHARD COLLIER sighed, grimaced. He glanced at his watch for the umpteenth time, and his irritation increased. Johnson, the woman from the coroner's office, had insisted that she see him that afternoon about the Twilly case. She had said she would be no later than three-thirty. Three-thirty had long since come and gone. It was now almost a quarter to five.

What in the world was keeping the woman?

And what was so important about the Twilly case? Why was she making such an issue of it? Why did she feel it was something she had to see him about in person?

Idly, Collier picked Twilly's medical profile off his desk and flipped it open. Wayne Twilly, sixteen years old, had been admitted to St. Mary's Mental Health Facility on January 25, three and a half weeks before. The admitting physician had written that the boy was suffering from "chronic insomnia and anxiety," and appeared to be "on the point of emotional collapse." After talking with the boy, Collier had concluded that the problem was far more severe. Collier's diagnosis had been "paranoid schizophrenic." In short, Wayne Twilly had been an individual so overpowered by his fears that he could no longer tell the difference between what was real and what was not.

Closing the folder, Collier visualized the young man: thin and pale, with deep, dark circles under his eyes—tired, drooping eyes that seemed forever on the verge of closing. When he spoke, it was in a soft weary monotone. And almost always, it was about the same thing—his dream. He had babbled endlessly about it.

"I'm not crazy, doctor," Twilly would say. "I don't belong here, in a mental hospital. There's nothing wrong with my mind, sir. That's not the problem. The problem is my dream. I just have a dream that's real."

Always the dream was the same. Twilly would describe himself as standing alone on a beach. At first everything was peaceful and beautiful. Then he became aware of a sound. A far-off rumbling. He looked up, looked out at the ocean and saw a wave—a giant black wall of seawater. It was in the distance, on the horizon. Slowly, very slowly, it was moving. Toward him. Each night—or whenever he slept—the wall of water got closer.

And there was no escaping it.

In his dream he would try to run. But he couldn't. No matter how hard he tried, he couldn't move his legs.

The wave was now almost on him, he said. Only inches away. And soon, he was sure, it would get him.

Explaining to the boy that it was only a dream did no good. Long therapy sessions had helped little. Group encounters had been useless. Nothing helped.

Wayne Twilly had gotten steadily worse.

He had become more withdrawn, more unreachable, more frightened. Finally, he had become so frightened— so afraid of his dream—that he had refused to sleep. He had fought it, had done everything to stay awake. For more than three days he had succeeded. Eyes glazed and heavy-lidded, for almost seventy-eight hours straight, he had paced the ward, a zombi-like creature mumbling that sleep was death.

It had been a terrible thing to see. Collier had felt so helpless, so useless. There had been nothing he could do.

And now he could do even less, except mull the whole thing over. And think and think and think . . .

Jarring Collier from his reverie, the intercom buzzed on his desk. Sylvia, Collier's secretary, announced that Ms. Johnson, from the coroner's office, had arrived.

"Send her in," he said. He let go of the intercom button. "About time," he muttered under his breath.

There was a knock at the door. It opened.

"Sorry to have kept you waiting," a heavy-set woman said as she hurried into the office.

"Quite all right," said Collier emptily. He pointed to a seat across from his desk.

The woman offered her excuses: a hectic day, problems at home, traffic.

"I understand," said Collier, trying to hide his impatience.

Ms. Johnson pulled a Manila folder from her briefcase. She opened it, leafed through pages. "Kindly tell me as much as you can about Wayne Twilly," she said, looking up from the folder.

"What can I tell you? Well, he was a nice kid. Terribly disturbed, but really a gentle soul. I liked him, and I feel awful about what's happened."

"That's not what I'm asking," said the woman.

"Oh?"

"Please, let's get to facts, to specifics."

"Of course."

She ran a hand through close-cropped hair. "Wayne Twilly is dead."

"Yes."

"And my job is to find out why."

"I understand," said Collier.

"What happened? What can you tell me about the boy and why he was here?"

Collier shifted in his seat. "He was schizophrenic. *Paranoid* schizophrenic. He didn't want to sleep."

"Why was that?"

"He was afraid of a nightmare he'd been having. Thought it was real. I was concerned about his health. I was worried not only about his mental well-being but his physical well-being. Getting almost no sleep was very hard on him."

"Without a doubt," said Ms. Johnson.

"I considered giving him something to make him sleep. However, under the circumstances, because of his fear of falling asleep, I did not want to give him anything without telling him first. I spoke to him about it, but he became very upset when I made the suggestion. He was in absolute terror. I didn't want to force the issue for fear of causing him to have a complete breakdown."

"I see," said the woman as she jotted a note in her folder. She looked up. "You say no sleep medication was prescribed?"

Collier shook his head.

"Was any medication, *of any sort*, given?"

"No."

She tapped a pencil against the folder. "How and when did Mr. Twilly fall asleep?"

"Wayne Twilly fell asleep about noon yesterday, on his own, in the ward." Collier made a face. "He was taken to his room. The next morning—at about 6:30 A.M.— we found him dead."

"I have the autopsy report here," said the woman. "And frankly, I find it baffling."

"In what way?" asked Collier, suddenly uneasy.

"Doesn't make any sense."

"What do you mean?"

"Mr. Twilly had water—seawater—in his lungs."

"What!" Collier blurted. "I don't understand."

"Neither do I," said the woman. "But the fact of the matter is that the cause of death in Mr. Twilly's case was drowning."

6
Captured on Canvas

IN HIS HEART, Hubert Morris knew that he was a great artist, a very special artist. He had a unique gift with brush and canvas. He was completely sure of it.

Despite the fact that he had never sold a single painting.

Humming contentedly, in the small back-room studio of his house, Hubert prepared for the painting he would do that day. With unhurried attention to detail, he arranged the subject of the painting: a still life, a crystal bowl filled with fruit. He pulled on a smock, set out his paints and brushes, set a fresh canvas on the easel. He squeezed blobs of vermilion, crimson, ocher, and willow green oil paint onto his palette. He added a bit of auburn, mixed it with a touch of white. For a long moment he locked his fishlike eyes, magnified hugely behind thick glasses, on the bowl of fruit. Filled with excitement, he poised his brush before the canvas. He began to paint.

"Oh, heavens!" he suddenly muttered.

Whiffers—his wife, Edwina's, spoiled, hateful poodle —was yapping to get in. He peered out the window. It had begun to drizzle. Whiffers was barking and scratching at the back door.

Setting aside his brush, Hubert made his way down the two stairs from his studio and, scowling, let the sodden, muddy little dog into the house. Soiling his smock, he carried Whiffers into the kitchen. "Nasty, dirty creature," he muttered as he wiped the dog with paper towels. He set Whiffers down. The dog scampered off down the hallway and immediately started yapping again, now to go back out. With a sigh, Hubert opened the door and let the dog dart out into the rain.

He returned to his study, to his painting.

Immediately Whiffers began to yip and yap—to get in.

"Oh, you horrid beast!" fretted Hubert. "Stay out there!" He slammed shut the door to his studio, pulled the drapes. He could still hear the muted barking of the dog. Looking about, he found a bit of cotton wool and stuffed some in each ear.

All was peaceful again, almost silent.

Humming, Hubert went back to work.

———

It was growing dark out when Hubert finally set his brushes down. With satisfaction, he studied his completed painting. It looked so real, so perfect.

He was cleaning up, putting things away when the studio door suddenly burst open. His wife, Edwina, soaking wet, stormed into the room. Her eyes blazed with anger and she was yelling. The words were muffled, indistinct.

Hubert pulled the cotton from his ears. "Hello, dear," he said.

"I've been knocking to get in for fifteen minutes! Couldn't find my house key! Searched everywhere for the spare. Fifteen minutes I've been out in the rain!"

"Sorry, dear."

"And what have you been doing all day?" she demanded. "Another one of your worthless paintings?"

"It's one of my best," beamed Hubert.

Her eyes fixed on his new picture. A sneer came to her mouth. "Gee, a bowl of fruit. How imaginative!"

"Thank you."

"I was being sarcastic, you nitwit."

"So was I, dear."

She aimed a finger at the painting. "Who'd ever want a picture like that? It's worthless."

"Not to me."

"All your pictures are of such stupid things. None of them are of anything anybody would want." She glanced about at the dozens of paintings on the studio walls. She pointed at a picture of a motorcycle. "Like that one, of that beat-up, noisy old motorbike that that kid next door used to race around the neighborhood on. Why would you paint something like that?"

"Because I enjoyed doing it."

"But who would buy such a painting?"

"My pictures aren't for sale, as you know."

"Because you know no one would want them."

Hubert shrugged.

"If you were a real man, a real artist, you'd do paintings you could sell. You'd be making some money from them, earning a living."

"We live comfortably. Mother's inheritance left us with more than enough to live as we choose, and I choose to paint."

"You're still living off your mother," she scoffed. "Lived with her until you were almost forty. And now you're still living in her house, living off her money."

"As you do."

She said nothing. Her mouth twisted into a sneer. She peered closer at the painting on the easel. "That's my good crystal bowl! Who said you could touch my bowl?"

Hubert's magnified eyes blinked.

"And where is it?" Her eyes darted around the room. "You'd better not have gotten paint on it—or lost it, like you did my candelabra!" She pulled off her wet raincoat, spattering Hubert, and strode angrily out of the room.

Hubert finished putting his things away. For a moment he studied his painting, admired it. He folded his smock neatly, laid it on a chair, and made his way reluctantly from his studio.

"Where is it?" groused Edwina, coming from the kitchen. "Where'd you put my bowl? Did you . . . ?"

She was cut off by a yapping and scratching outside. "Whiffers!" she cried, pulling open the back door.

The rain-drenched poodle bounded into the room.

"Oh, my poor baby!" exclaimed the woman. She hurried into the bathroom, quickly returned with a towel. "Mommy's poor dear babykins," she cooed, wrapping Whiffers in the towel. "You've got the shiver-whivers." She hugged the sopping dog to her, kissed it, nuzzled it. "My poor sweetie!" She looked up, glowered angrily at Hubert.

He backed away.

"How could you!" she demanded. "You left my Whiffers out in the rain!"

"He wanted to go out," said Hubert meekly.

"All day! And in this rain and cold!"

"Sorry," said Hubert.

"Be quiet!" growled Edwina, making her way into the bathroom with the towel-wrapped poodle. Water pipes squawked and screeched, water gurgled into the bathtub. "Mommy give poor baby a nice hot bath," she babbled to her dog. "The bad man was mean to you, wasn't he?"

The dog barked its agreement.

"Oh, brother!" groaned Hubert under his breath.

The days that followed were unpleasant ones. Whiffers had come down with a case of the sniffles. Edwina's crystal bowl had not yet turned up, though she had looked high and low for it. And to make matters worse, Hubert, on his way from the garage to his studio, had spilled a bottle of linseed oil on the hall carpet, leaving an ugly yellow stain.

Edwina alternated between fits of screaming and long hours of frosty silence.

Hubert promised he would make it all up to her.

"And how are you going to do that?" she demanded.

"A surprise. A nice surprise for you."

"I can hardly wait," she scoffed.

"No, really. You'll be pleased. It's a picture."

"Of what?"

"You'll see," he said with a timid smile, and hurried off to his studio.

Returning home from the beauty parlor one afternoon, Edwina was greeted by Hubert's announcement that his surprise for her was ready. Grudgingly, she followed him into his studio. On the wall hung a new picture, covered with a draping of pink velvet.

"Close your eyes," he said, pinching the velvet between thumb and forefinger.

"Don't be a child," she grumped. "Uncover it."

Hubert shrugged, then, with a smile, unveiled the picture.

"Oh, I love it!" she exclaimed. "Oh, you finally did something good, something worthwhile! A picture of Whiffers!"

"Really like it?" he asked.

She planted a wet kiss on his cheek. "That really *is* a nice surprise!" She examined the picture from all angles. "It looks just like him." She touched the glass covering the picture. "Ooh, it looks so real, like he could just jump right out at you, doesn't it?"

"Yes," he grinned.

Edwina bustled out of the room. "I've got to show Whiffers his picture!" she said gleefully.

"Naturally," said Hubert.

The back door opened. "Whiffers baby," called Edwina. "Whiffers dearest, come and see the picture Daddy painted of you!"

Hubert followed her to the open door.

"Whiffers! Come to Mommy." She trudged out into the backyard. "Whiffers, where are you? Whiffers?" A puzzled look on her face, she circled the yard, then hurried back to the house. "Where is he?" she said worriedly, pushing past Hubert.

"I'm sure he's around here someplace."

"Whiffers!" she called over and over, tromping from room to room. "Whiffers!"

"I wonder where he could be," mused Hubert, following on her heels.

She wheeled on him. "You've done something to him, haven't you?" she shrieked. "Is this your idea of a joke? You give me a picture of my baby, then get rid of him?"

"No, of course not," protested Hubert.

"So help me, if you did anything to that dog!" Edwina pulled open the front door. "Whiffers!" she called, making her way down the front steps and out to the sidewalk. She headed off down the street, calling the dog's name over and over.

A week passed. Then two. A trip to the animal shelter turned up nothing. Edwina posted signs all over the neighborhood. She went door to door.

But there was no trace of the missing dog.

"I'm sure he'll turn up," Hubert reassured her one afternoon upon her return from another fruitless search of the neighborhood.

"No, he won't," she sniffed. "I'll never see him again!" She hung her head, daubed at her eyes with a handkerchief. She looked up. A sorrowful expression suddenly changed to one of hate. "It's you!" she blurted, aiming a finger at him. "I know it! What did you do? You beast, you did something to my Whiffers."

"Nonsense, my dear."

"Nonsense, nothing! You did something."

"Such as?"

"You never liked Whiffers."

"I adored him."

"Liar! You did not!"

"I did so. Didn't I paint his picture?"

She advanced on him. "You, you're the one!" she yelled. "You got rid of him!"

Hubert retreated.

She was circling him now, shaking a fist in his face. "What did you do?"

"Nothing." He backed away, then hurried off down the hall.

"You come back here!" yelled Edwina. "I'm not done with you yet!" She stormed down the hall after him.

Hubert pushed into his studio and, with a loud sigh, locked the door behind him.

The knob rattled. A fist pounded on the door. "You come out of there!" screamed Edwina.

"No."

"Come out!"

"Please leave me in peace," he begged.

"You open this door!" she demanded.

"Go away."

"Not until you tell me what you've done. Tell me!"

"Leave me alone or I'll—"

"Or you'll *what*?"

Hubert made no reply.

"You're a freak! There's something strange about you. Something about those paintings you do in there."

Hubert nodded yes, smiled to himself. He looked about at the many pictures on his studio walls. Each was a silent testimonial to his gift, his special talent. Captured on canvas was the ugly crystal bowl he had always hated. Whiffers was up there, too. And so was old Simon Willowby, greedy old Willowby, who had talked Hubert into investing in stocks in a nonexistent oil well—and had "disappeared" with the money.

"What are you doing?" demanded Edwina.

Hubert was admiring his painting of the motorcycle, the noisy old motorcycle that had belonged to the kid next door—until it too had "disappeared."

"Open this door!" demanded Edwina. "Or so help me I'll make your life miserable."

"You already do," said Hubert.

"Oh, I do, do I?"

Hubert said nothing. Quietly, he set about arranging his paints and brushes, then setting a fresh canvas on the easel.

"You let me in!"

Humming to himself, Hubert began work on a new picture, a portrait.

"You can't stay in there forever. And when you come out, I'll be waiting for you!"

"No, you won't," said Hubert. His gaze returned to the walls of his studio, to his paintings, his private gallery of unwanted people, unwanted things. The only problem: There was so little space left. He would have to make some changes, he decided. Some of the other paintings would have to be moved around a bit—to make a place to put Edwina.

7
Class Reunion

DENNIS EMERSON WIPED sweat from his brow, switched on the car air conditioner. He blinked against the glare of the mid-September sun, glanced at his watch as he drove. Nineteen minutes to eight. In the morning. It was hot, too hot for so early in the morning. Too hot for the first day of class. By afternoon, the classrooms would be broiling.

Emerson loosened his tie. He flipped on the car radio, and in the next instant, irritably turned off the grating babble of a commercial. And again glanced at his watch.

He was nervous.

After four years of teaching, the first day of class should not have bothered him at all. First day jitters were something he had long ago conquered. Or so he had thought.

But now Emerson was coming home to teach. He was back in Banyon, Vermont. His old home town. And back at his old school.

James Madison High School loomed ahead, the two-story brick buildings looking as solid and dreary as when Emerson had graduated from the place. More than nine years ago.

No, he decided as he pulled into the faculty parking lot. *No, the place hasn't changed a bit.*

Nothing had changed.

Except now he was a teacher, not a student.

Despite his earlier nervousness, Emerson's first four classes, three U.S. History and one U.S. Government, went smoothly. Like a breeze. The kids, after all, were just kids. A little restless after a summer off. A little anxious on the first day of school. Quiet, for the most part, sizing him up. He joked a bit. Outlined the course of study, then told a little about his background. About his years at Missouri State University, and his earlier teaching positions. Even about how—"in prehistoric times"—he had attended Madison High.

The students fanned themselves with folders and handmade fans as he spoke.

All in all, Emerson was able to ignore the heat. Sure, he was too warm, and his shirt collar was open and his tie hanging loose and limp, but he was too busy getting the new semester underway to let it really bother him.

Emerson's first four classes were in the Social Sciences wing, in room 117. His last class of the day, after lunch and his break period, was an English course, in the Language Arts wing. In room 502.

He hated the number.

He hated the room.

He knew it all too well. Room 502 brought back painful memories. Ugly memories. Ones he had never shared with anyone.

And never would.

A bell sounded, ending his break period. In the faculty lounge and rest room, he patted his face with a moistened paper towel. He focused his mind on the task ahead, and snatching up his briefcase, headed out from the lounge and across campus to the Language Arts wing.

To room 502.

He was sweating and out of breath as he made his way up the stairs and unlocked the door. Students shuffled in behind him. Chairs squeaked. Notebooks thumped on desks. Kids settled into seats, looked at him as he set down his briefcase and clicked it open. He glanced at the class roster, noted with satisfaction that only twenty-four students were enrolled. All his other classes had over thirty. One had forty-one.

Emerson gestured to two boys in the back of the room.

"Gentlemen," he said, "let's open some windows. It's pretty darn hot and stuffy in here."

Without comment, the boys opened the windows.

The starting bell sounded.

Emerson wrote his name on the board. He smiled out at the class, cleared his throat. "Welcome, everyone," he began. "I am Mr. Emerson, and this is Senior Composition. Doesn't sound too exciting, but we'll give it a chance. I have a hunch we can make it a lot more interesting—and fun—than it sounds." Another smile. He settled into his seat behind his desk.

The class was quiet, too quiet. All eyes were on him.

"So let's get things going." He pulled a pen from his pocket and smoothed the class roster before him on his desk. "Let me know if you're out there when I call your name."

He pushed on reading glasses, called the first name on the roll sheet. A hand raised. "Here," said a heavy-set boy, as the door suddenly squawked open and a straggler hurried in. A blonde girl mumbled an apology, made her way to a vacant seat. Emerson caught a quick glimpse of her. And then she melded in behind other faces.

For some reason she made him feel uneasy.

He resumed calling roll. The straggler's name was the next one on the roster. He stared at the name: *Mary Cummings.* A twinge of fear hit Emerson. His voice trembling slightly, he called her name.

The answering voice was a familiar one.

Emerson craned his neck, glanced over his reading glasses. An unspeakable sense of dread gripped him. His gaze locked on the petite, brown-eyed blonde in the back of the room.

He had seen her before, or so it seemed. Had known her. Long ago.

Just coincidence, he told himself. *Your mind's playing tricks on you.* He mopped his brow, tried to collect his thoughts.

All was silent. Students were waiting for him to continue. They stared at him, and looked from one to the other, puzzled expressions on their faces.

"Are you okay, sir?" asked a boy.

"Yes," muttered Emerson. And then he saw the face connected to the voice. It was a face he remembered, a face from long ago: dark, gaunt, thin-lipped. And nearby there was another familiar face. A pale, gentle face. Close-cropped hair, wire-rimmed glasses.

Emerson fought the mounting terror within him. *Get hold of yourself*, a voice screamed inside his head. He took a deep breath, continued to call the names on the roster. He knew two of the names before he got to them, those of the boys with the all-too-familiar faces: James Winston and Brian Young.

Emerson's voice was no more than a warbling, off-pitch, unsteady slur by the time he had completed taking roll. His mind was blank. Desperately he tried to think.

His usual introductory talk was out of the question.

Any sort of the usual ice-breaking banter was beyond him.

He licked dry lips. "I would like to learn a little about your writing skills," he said hesitantly, "and learn a little about you." He cleared his throat noisily. "For your first assignment, please write a brief, two-page autobiography."

Amidst groans and sour looks, notebooks popped open. Pens and papers were produced.

"Please double-space and use proper paragraph form," said Emerson, his voice breathy, cracking.

"Are you sure you're okay, sir?" asked James Winston.

For a long moment Emerson said nothing. He stared at the boy. "No," muttered Emerson. "No, I'm afraid I don't feel very well."

"I understand," said Winston. "I understand completely, sir."

Pens scratched on paper. Occasionally there was a cough or the sound of a chair screeching on linoleum.

Emerson sat tensely, his shirt wet with perspiration. He watched his students as they worked. All new faces —except three.

He looked up at the clock on the wall. The minute hand clicked back, clicked forward. Six to three. Over. Almost over, he told himself.

"Five minutes," he announced. Many of the kids were already done, sitting quietly. A few faces looked up, then went back to work. He took a deep breath, settled back in his chair. Tried to relax.

He was gazing out the window, deep in thought.

A door rattled open behind him, startling him. The students looked up. Everyone was looking in the direction of the door—except Mary Cummings, James Winston, and Brian Young. Their eyes were fixed on their teacher—waiting, watching.

Emerson knew whom he would see—before he turned, as he turned.

Rusty Simmons was a tall, gangly redhead. A bookworm with wavy red hair, an easy smile, and dark brown eyes that seemed to forever gaze at the world in awe and wonder.

Emerson stared in horror.

Rusty handed him an enrollment card. "I'm sorry I'm late, sir," he said softly. "I was talking to my counselor. I wanted to make sure I got your class."

Emerson fumbled for words. "How can this be happening?" he blurted.

"Pardon me, sir?" asked Rusty.

"Why are you here?"

"Don't you know, sir?"

The class stared. Mary Cummings, Brian Young, and James Winston grinned.

Emerson rose shakily to his feet. "How can you be here? How can *they* be here?" He pointed at Mary, Brian, and James.

Rusty said nothing.

Emerson backed away. "You're dead!" he screamed, lurching toward the door. "The four of you! Dead!"

He never bothered to sign out.

Terrified, he had gone home, to his small apartment.

The place was hot, stuffy. Mostly he sat in front of the TV. Seeing nothing. Unable to concentrate—on anything.

From time to time he leaned back, parted dusty venetian blinds, peered out at a darkening street.

Then he returned to staring at TV.

Finally, he turned it off.

All was silent.

From outside came footsteps. And then a knocking at the door. Numb, unsteadily he made his way from the sofa. To the door. He opened it a crack.

"Mr. Emerson?"

Sarah Seymore, Madison's principal, was standing on the stoop.

"Mr. Emerson?" she said again.

"Yes?"

"I would have called, but . . ."

"My phone isn't connected yet." He ran a hand through his hair, tried to straighten his rumpled suit, the same one he had worn since that morning. "Please come in," he said, his voice a dull monotone.

"Mr. Emerson—Dennis—what happened? What happened today?" Seymore asked, after they had both made their way into the small living room and taken seats.

Emerson said nothing.

"You came to us highly recommended," said the fortyish woman. "I was pleased to have you. Your reputation preceded you. But today, I'm told, you left your classroom before the period ended. Your students were out in the halls. Students came to my office and said you'd run out of class—ran out yelling, and in great distress. Is this correct?"

He nodded, his eyes downcast.

"Would you care to tell me why?"

"You wouldn't understand." He shrugged. "I'm not even sure *I* understand."

"Mr. Emerson, what's going on?"

"I don't know."

"Possibly I can help."

"No, no one can." He shook his head slowly from side to side.

"Let me try." She smiled. "Mr. Emerson—Dennis—what's wrong, what is it?"

"It's all so insane. You won't believe me."

"Believe *what*?"

His head slowly swiveled toward her. "There are four students in my last period class, four students I went to school with."

"Pardon me?"

"I went to school with them at Madison. When I was a kid, I went to school with them. The same names, the same faces. The same four kids: Mary Cummings, James Winston, Brian Young, and Rusty Simmons."

"Mr. Emerson, that's not possible."

"Regardless, it's true. They were my classmates nine years ago. Only they haven't aged a day."

"Surely, Mr. Emerson, you're imagining—"

"No," he said, interrupting her. "I'm not imagining anything." He looked at her sorrowfully. "You see, they've come back for me."

"Come back for you? What do you mean?"

"What I mean, Ms. Seymore, is that they're dead. And I killed them."

The woman stared, a look of shock on her face. "You *killed them?*"

"Not on purpose. It was an accident." He looked down, clutched the knees of wrinkled trousers. He looked up. "A Pontiac GTO. A classic. A '67. Light blue. Landau top. Mag wheels and—"

"Mr. Emerson," interrupted the woman, "what are you talking about?"

"Nine years ago I sold that car to Rusty Simmons, a kid in my Expository Writing Class, room 502. The guy didn't know a thing about cars, never even had it checked out. Just paid what I was asking for it."

"What are you trying to say?"

"The car needed a new brake cylinder—a master cylinder. I knew it, but Rusty didn't. And I didn't want to shell out the two hundred or so it would take to fix it." He grimaced. "And if I'd told him the repairs it needed, he wouldn't have bought the car, not at the price I was asking.

"That evening—the evening he picked up the car—he went for a ride. And he took his friends—James Winston, Brian Young, and Mary Cummings. They headed up into the Snake Mountains. They went up the old road, and along Dead Man's Curve. The brakes failed."

"And they were killed?" asked Sarah Seymore.

"Yes, all of them. All four—Mary, James, Brian, and Rusty." He ran tense fingers through his hair. "All four."

Shaken, at a loss for words, Sarah Seymore rose to her feet. "We'll talk tomorrow," she said. "We need to talk. We—"

He shook his head. "I won't be in tomorrow."

For a moment the woman stared. "Oh," was all she managed to say.

He looked away.

The woman pursed her lips. "I'll show myself out," she said.

Emerson nodded.

He closed his aching eyes.

His mind drifted. He dozed. Fitfully.

When he awoke, it was with a painful crink in his neck. He felt sluggish, and a bit dizzy. And he was bathed in a cold sweat. He glanced at his watch. 9:20. Almost two hours had passed.

Yawning, he sat up, wiped his brow on his sleeve.

Idly, he parted the blinds. A shock wave of fear hit him. At the curb, in the otherwise empty street, was a Pontiac. Light blue. Landau top. Mag wheels.

Heart racing, he rushed out the door. And into the street. He looked up and down the block. No one was around. Tentatively he approached the car. He walked around it, studied it. Mag wheels. Quad headlights. Louver-style taillights.

The car he had sold to Rusty Simmons.

"No," he muttered. "Can't be. Can't be happening."

He wanted to get away. Had to.

He turned to head back across the street.

"Super car, isn't it, sir?" said a voice behind him.

He stopped. Woodenly, he turned.

They were there.

Mary Cummings was sitting on the fender, Brian beside her. James Winston stood with his arms folded across his chest. Rusty was polishing the chrome-rimmed side mirror.

"How do you like my car, sir?" asked Rusty.

"It's a beauty, isn't it?" said Mary.

Emerson stood riveted in place, staring in horror.

"We're going for a spin," said Rusty.

"Know where we're headed?" asked Brian.

Emerson's mouth opened. No words came from him.

"Dead Man's Curve! Snake Mountains!" exclaimed Brian. "Up the old road."

"You should join us," said Mary, sliding off the fender.

Rusty's arm went around Emerson's shoulder. "You look unhappy, sir. A little ride, I'll bet, is just what you need."

Emerson tried to back away. Rusty's arm clutched him tightly. Brian Young clamped hold of his wrist. Mary took his hand.

James Winston opened the car door.

"Come on, sir," said Rusty. "Come with us. Join us."

"No!" cried Emerson, his whole body trembling, rubbery, his legs weak, buckling under him. "Please, no!"

Rusty and Brian gripped him, kept him from falling. Held him tightly. Guided him. And helped him toward the open door of the car.

8
The Hunted

KURT DOBLER WAS ANGRY. He had planned the hunting trip down to the last detail. But now Milton, his fool of a cousin, was fouling up the works, messing up the schedule.

Milton was to have arrived at Kurt's house no later than 3:00 A.M. That would have given them plenty of time to pack the Land Rover and be on the road before four, four-thirty at the latest.

Already the sky was tinged with gold. It would soon be dawn. Milton was over an hour late.

Waiting for Milton, fuming, Dobler packed the gear into the Land Rover himself. It was the heavy gear, all the important items: the tents, tarp, cooler, skinning knives, rifles, and a hundred rounds of ammunition. He made one last check of everything, then headed into the house, into the kitchen. He poured himself a cup of coffee, then dialed Milton's number. The phone was ringing unanswered as a car—Milton's old Buick—pulled up out in front.

Dobler went to the front door. He stood sipping his coffee as Milton made his way up the walkway.

"Good morning, Kurt," said Milton.

"You're late!" snapped Dobler.

Milton looked at his watch. "Yeah, a bit I guess. Sorry." He glanced out at the street. "But so are Bob and Tyler and Ed."

"For crying out loud! I told you last week Ed isn't coming, and Bob Pelton and Tyler Bates are driving up on their own. They won't be getting to the campsite until late this afternoon, maybe not until tonight."

"Gee, I don't remember you telling me that, Kurt."

"Don't you ever get anything straight?"

Milton's face reddened a bit. He shrugged sheepishly.

"Get your junk loaded into the Rover," ordered Dobler. Leaving the door ajar, he made his way into the den. He sat down with his coffee. He pulled out a map and began studying it.

A few minutes later, Milton made his way into the house. "My stuff's all in the Rover, Kurt," he said.

Dobler made no response. He continued studying the map.

Uneasy, Milton waited, nervously shifting his weight

74

from foot to foot. Then quietly he began wandering about the den. His eyes were filled with awe. On the floor there was a bearskin rug. And heads were seemingly everywhere. The heads of elk, deer, moose, and other animals decorated the walls. "You sure are some hunter, Kurt," he said.

Dobler looked up.

"You're the best," said Milton.

Dobler nodded his agreement.

"Me, I don't have anything on my walls. Not a single deer. Nothin'. Me, I'm not quite up in your league, yet."

Dobler smiled crookedly. "Think you ever will be?"

Milton made a face, said nothing.

Dobler took a last sip of coffee. He folded up the map, pushed himself to his feet. "Let's get going," he said.

Milton pulled on a hunting cap. He hurried to catch up to Dobler, who was already headed out the door.

By midafternoon they were deep into the White Mountains. They had long ago left the highway. Trees towered overhead, and the Land Rover bucked and jolted along a narrow dirt road, leaving a great plume of dust in its wake.

"Hang on!" chuckled Dobler. He down-shifted and pumped the brakes as he turned off the road and headed down a steeply inclined grass-covered slope. The Land Rover rocked and swayed, crunched through dry brush and kicked up clumps of grass as it descended into a deep valley. "Am I scarin' ya?" sneered Dobler, glancing with a hard smile at Milton.

The man stared straight ahead, a white-knuckled death grip on the dashboard.

The land leveled off. Dobler hit the brakes, brought the Rover to a scudding stop. He pulled on the hand brake and swung his heavy, muscular frame from the vehicle. Stuffing keys into his pocket, he surveyed the scene. They were in a meadow, surrounded on all sides by vast forests shrouded in an odd, amber-colored mist.

"I've heard," said Milton, "that these mountains are supposed to be haunted. They were sacred to the Indians. And the spirits of the Indians, or something, it's said, still protect the animals."

"Garbage," scoffed Dobler.

"Well, now, Scott Morsley over at the garage says people have just plain disappeared in these woods. And all sorts of other strange things are said to have happened."

"Gee, you got me shakin' in my boots."

"I'm just repeating what Scott Morsley told me."

"Morsley's an idiot. Told me the same stupid thing." Dobler made his way to the back of the Rover, Milton on his heels. He tossed a blanket, a packet of dried fruit, and a bottle of water into a backpack. He pulled on a well-worn army jacket, stuffed the pockets with ammunition. He slid a Mauser MI-898 rifle from its case, checked the bolt action.

"What are you doing?" asked Milton.

"Going to head out, scout the land. Meantime, you set up the tents, get things in order. Bob and Tyler should be arriving within the next couple of hours."

Milton shrugged. "Okay, you're the boss," he said.

The sunlit meadow gave way to thick brush and to a seemingly topless world of majestic trees. Dobler felt good. He felt powerful and strong as he trudged through the forest. The only sound was of his heavy footsteps, of birds chattering and wind whistling eerily through the conifers and elms. As he walked, he studied the ground. There were deer droppings, and the soil was pounded and pocked by hoofprints. He smiled with satisfaction, continued on, along a rocky ledge skirting a deep gorge. Shouldering his rifle, he clambered over a huge fallen tree. He pulled his way up through high grass, then made his way along the winding crest line of a mountain.

He glanced at his watch. Almost five-thirty. It was growing late. There was a decided chill in the air, and the sun was sinking beneath a distant ridge, streaking the forest with long lavender shadows. It would be dark out soon. For a moment, Dobler paused. He could head back to the campsite—or keep going. Briefly, he thought of Milton, and of the others, who by now had surely arrived.

They could fend for themselves, he decided.

He picked his way down a slope thickly carpeted with pine needles. The sound of rushing water greeted his ears, grew louder as he lumbered down the mountainside. Ahead, through the trees, he spotted a waterfall—several of them, really. A granite cliff had been worn away into what looked like four or five close-together chimneys. Water gushed over them, spilled down them, into a lake.

And lapping at the water's edge was a small doe.

Dobler unshouldered his rifle. Smiling, he sighted quickly, expertly. Too late, the doe turned, its soft brown eyes filled with fear. Dobler fired. The animal crumpled to the ground.

There was a shout—a scream of protest. It sounded human.

Dobler looked about. He turned.

An old man was standing behind him.

Startled, Dobler jumped involuntarily. "Where did you come from?" he demanded, his voice quavering.

The man, an Indian, it seemed, said nothing. His eyes were fixed on Dobler. The eyes looked black, lifeless. His hair was white, his face a brown webwork of wrinkles. A necklace of bone was about his neck.

"Who are you? Where'd you come from?" Dobler again demanded.

The old man looked at the deer. "You have killed this helpless creature. Did you think it was without feeling?

Did you think it would not feel the pain of your bullet?"

"It's nothing but a stupid animal."

"Have you no love in your heart, no understanding?"

Dobler aimed a finger at the man. "Get out of my face!"

"A man such as you does not belong here."

"Is that right?"

"This is a sacred place, a holy place," said the man. "A place of the magic of life. You have defiled it by your act of treachery. You reek of evil."

"Beat it, Geronimo!"

The man knelt beside the deer. He touched its head gently and began to chant softly.

"What are you supposed to be, some sort of stupid medicine man?"

The old man put his hands in the blood of the deer. He rose, and startling Dobler, suddenly pressed his bloodied hands to Dobler's face.

"What!" growled Dobler. He grabbed the old man by the shirt and pushed him sprawling to the ground. "Get out of here!"

The old man struggled to his feet. He raised his arms, extended his reddened hands. Blood began to spill from splayed fingers, then to pour from them. He touched his hands together. And they were suddenly clean, free of blood.

"What'd you do?" Dobler blurted, the hair standing up on the back of his neck.

The old man's black eyes widened. An eerie darkness gathered about him. It encompassed him, and obscured him. He seemed to recede into it.

And then he was gone.

"Where are you?" screamed Dobler, backing away. He tripped, fell. Shaken, he stared where the figure had been. He crawled to the lake. He scooped up water and tried to wash the blood from his face. His skin continued to feel sticky. Again he scooped up water, again wiped at his face. He took a swallow of water. Gagging, he spat it out. It tasted of blood.

Rank and strong. Thick, sickeningly sweet. Like blood.

"Just your imagination," he muttered under his breath, lurching to his feet, backing away. He looked around, then hurried back up the slope. He found a trail, broke into a trot, a run.

Night was falling.

He could hardly see his feet.

He tripped over something, stumbled. Continued on. He stopped. He realized he had lost the trail. He looked about. He pushed his way through heavy brush, entered a clearing and tossed his pack and gun to the ground. "Won't be the first night I slept in the woods," he mumbled to himself.

With trembling hands, he fumbled about in the half-dark, gathered up small branches and handfuls of pine needles. Soon he had a fire going. An icy wind blew out of the north. Wrapping himself in his blanket, he curled up beside the fire. Flickering shadows danced about him in the dark forest. He felt ill. Strange. He closed his eyes. An overpowering weariness settled over him. His mind drifted. He slept.

A bright morning sun was beating down, searing through his eyelids.

Something was wrong. He felt odd. His heart pounding, Kurt Dobler opened his eyes.

He looked down at his arms. But he no longer had any. Instead, where arms should have been, he had legs. Where he had once had hands, there were hooves. His feet, too, were hooves. And everywhere he was covered with a coarse, tan hide. Echoing screams filled his head.

He struggled to all fours. In horror, he looked about, then hurried down to the lake. Fearfully, slowly, he made his way into shallow water. He stopped. He lowered his head, gazed down at the reflected image.

Of a deer.

His once sharp blue eyes had turned timid and brown. His neck was long. His ears pointed. And a great pair of antlers grew from his head.

Again came the screaming inside his head.

His own voice.

And that of an animal.

An animal in pain.

He ran along the damp, sandy shoreline of the lake, surprised at his fleetness of foot. He clambered over a berm, hooves clattering on the stones underfoot. He pushed through brush, found a trail, and loped along it beneath massive pines. The trail widened. He broke into a run.

Panting, he reached the crest of a hill. He paused, rested, gazed ahead. In the far distance he could make out his Rover and a pickup, and two tents, and with a keen sense of smell, detected the scent of burning wood.

The campsite.

Milton was there. And so were the others. Somehow they would help him.

And end the horror.

He made his way down the hill, through dense woods that opened onto a rolling meadow. He loped across the vast, grassy field toward the camp. He slowed to a walk, entered a stand of trees.

Suddenly he stopped—at the sound of men's voices. Bob Pelton was stooped over a fire. Milton emerged from a tent, followed by Tyler Bates.

Seeing his cousin and friends lifted Dobler's spirits. He made his way out into the open and timidly approached them. "Help me!" he tried to cry.

But a deer has no voice; not a word came from him.

"Look at that buck!" yelled Bob Pelton.

"And comin' right to us!" exclaimed Bates, grabbing a rifle from the cab of his pickup.

"No!" Dobler tried to scream. "I'm your friend!"

Bates sighted. Fired.

The bullet grazed Dobler's shoulder, sent a searing pain through him. He stumbled. Ran.

Another shot rang out.

He started back through the stand of trees. Then out into the open. Across the meadow.

Somewhere behind him an engine roared to life. Men yelled. Laughed. Tires squealed.

In agony, Dobler looked back, struggled on.

Behind him, the pickup rattled and bounced across the meadow. A volley of shots cracked the morning air. Bullets thudded into the ground, ricocheted off rock. A shotgun roared.

Dobler reeled as a pellet stung him, burned into him.

"Get him!" shouted one of the men.

The pickup was almost alongside. Dobler veered, rushed headlong into the forest. He forced himself on, struggled along beneath a canopy of trees.

"Please! No!" he tried to cry.

The pickup had fishtailed to a shuddering halt. The hunters leaped from it and, rifles in hand, raced heavy-footed into the woods and after their prey.

Shots snapped branches, kicked up puffs of dust.

He plunged onward, ever deeper into the forest, the hunters in noisy pursuit.

"Where'd he go?" questioned a voice somewhere behind.

Gasping, he headed down into a deep valley. He moved cautiously, seeking a place to hide, listening carefully for the sound of the men.

It seemed he had lost them. He slowed his gait. He crossed a small stream, moved deeper into the valley. He paused to rest, to let the pain in his shoulder subside, to gather air into his oxygen-starved lungs. Huffing, he continued on, at a trot. Then at a walk. All was silent. His head turned. He looked back. He hurried on. His gaze shifted ahead, then up. He stared in horror. He was in a box canyon. Ahead—and on both sides—loomed sheer cliffs.

He was trapped!

He turned, began to run, back the way he had come.

"I see him!" someone suddenly yelled.

He stopped, stood frozen, stared about in panic. Footsteps approached through the forest. His soft brown eyes became bright with fear.

"This way!" yelled another voice.

Down a slope, stones clattered, bounded and bounced. Soil hissed, cascaded downward. Out of breath, Bob Pelton and Tyler Bates came scrambling down a hillside.

He ran, into the woods. Then slowed.

More footsteps. Ahead. Coming toward him.

A figure emerged from the trees. It was Milton.

The man's mouth opened wide. A rifle was cocked. Raised to shoulder level.

Frantic, Dobler rose on hind legs. "No!" he tried to scream. "You don't understand! Don't do this to me!"

Milton sighted. The gun roared, roared again . . .

Kurt Dobler was never seen again.

It was a mystery to Milton, Tyler Bates, and Bob Pelton.

One evening, Milton invited his friends over to his house. Excited, eager, he led them down to his game room.

"Looks great!" exclaimed Tyler Bates.

"Picked it up today," said Milton. He pointed with pride at the mounted head of a deer above his fireplace. The head was huge, beautiful, the antlers so large they almost touched the ceiling.

"A beauty," said Bob Pelton.

"Boy, if that isn't the truth!" said Bates admiringly.

Milton beamed. "My first kill!"

"Too bad Kurt isn't here," said Bates.

"Yeah," agreed Pelton. "He would have been really impressed."

"Think so?" asked Milton.

"Yeah, and probably a bit jealous," said Bates. "Even he never got a deer like this one."

Horror Stories
Supernatural